Natasha Rejoices in Life!

"I've seen Natasha's audiences burst into laughter, cheers, and applause at her verse. She captures the hopes and aspii much a part of modern wom captures it all with marvelot
— *Washington Post*

"Every minute you spend with Natasha gives you laughter, pleasure and new insights."
— Spencer Johnson, M.D., co-author of *The One Minute Manager* and author of *One Minute for Myself*

"Absolutely wonderful, beautiful, exciting, economical, witty, targeted, relevant, sensual, worldly."
— Claire Donovan, Associate Dean of Medicine, University of Texas Medical Branch, Galveston

"Natasha Josefowitz's poetry is OUTSTANDING!!!!"
— Marcia G. Davis, Executive Director, Personal Best Workshops for Achievement and Personal Growth, Pinellas Park, Florida

"Natasha has another winner on her hands. It is delightful to enjoy her poems and feel validated, laugh, and be understood all at the same time. The humor, the hopefulness, the surprises ... go straight to the heart and gut, a double impact."
— Lee Gardenswartz, Ph.D., Training and Consulting Associates, Marina Del Rey, California

Also by Natasha Josefowitz

IS THIS WHERE I WAS GOING? *
              (light verse)
PATHS TO POWER: A Woman's Guide from
              First Job to Top Executive
YOU'RE THE BOSS! A Guide to Managing
              People with Understanding
              and Effectiveness *

*published by Warner Books.

NATASHA'S WORDS FOR FAMILIES

NATASHA JOSEFOWITZ

DRAWINGS BY
MARY MIETZELFELD

WARNER BOOKS

A Warner Communications Company

This book is part of a trilogy. The other two
by the same author are:

Natasha's Words for Lovers
Natasha's Words for Friends

Copyright © 1986 by Natasha Josefowitz
All rights reserved.
Warner Books, Inc., 666 Fifth Avenue, New York, NY 10103
W A Warner Communications Company
Printed in the United States of America
First Printing: November 1986
10 9 8 7 6 5 4 3

Cover design by Mary Mietzelfeld

Library of Congress Cataloging-in-Publication Data

Josefowitz, Natasha.
    Natasha's words for families.

    1. Family — Poetry. I. Title. II. Title: Words for
families.
PS3560.0768N3 1986   811'.54   86-9243
ISBN 0-446-38297-3 (U.S.A.) (pbk.)
        0-446-38298-1 (Canada) (pbk.)

ATTENTION: SCHOOLS AND CORPORATIONS

Warner books are available at quantity discounts with bulk purchase for educational,
business, or sales promotional use. For information, please write to: Special Sales
Department, Warner Books, 666 Fifth Avenue, New York, NY 10103.

**ARE THERE WARNER BOOKS YOU WANT
BUT CANNOT FIND IN YOUR LOCAL STORES?**

You can get any Warner Books title in print. Simply send title and retail price, plus 50¢ per
order and 50¢ per copy to cover mailing and handling costs for each book desired. New
York State and California residents, add applicable sales tax. Enclose check or money
order—no cash, please—to: **Warner Books, PO Box 690, New York, NY 10019**. Or send for
our complete catalog of Warner Books.

To my daughter Nina with much love.

A special thanks to my late grandparents and father, to my mother, my brother, my husband, my children, children-in-law, stepchildren, grandchildren, step-grandchildren, my in-laws, nieces, nephews, cousins, aunts and uncles, all of whom contributed to this book by being such a wonderful and diverse family.

While some of the verses are autobiographical, many reflect the feelings and experiences of friends and colleagues. I am grateful for their sharing them with me and making this book richer.

Contents

Introduction

This book is written for parents and for children because families provide what no friend can — no matter how seldom we see one another, how different we may have become, among us there is always a room ready when it is needed, someone from whom to seek advice or help, or a caring person to share in the special events.

We may meet only at weddings and at funerals, but the unspoken closeness is always there. To parents and children everywhere, may these bonds endure forever.

The Homemaker

The laundry is not folded right
the shirts are left unironed
the beds are always made with lumps
the books are never dusted

The glasses are never dried by hand
the sofa does not get vacuumed
hard-to-reach shelves are never cleaned
the closets are left messy

The windowpanes seldom get washed
the coffee is always instant
the dining table has a vinyl cloth
we're using paper napkins

My husband just doesn't keep house
according to my mother's standards.

No Time

No time to market
too busy to cook
too tired to go out for dinner

Frozen pizza again tonight!

Someday I'll Have Time

Someday,
I will be able to
read the latest novels
go to the theater
walk on the beach
visit with friends
attend lectures
go to exhibits
take long vacations
cook gourmet meals
throw lavish parties

so I'll put this book
on the shelf
and clip this recipe
for the file
send for the travel folder...

when I have time.

Stop the World

Stop the world
I want to get off
I want to leave my desk
so piled up with papers
I cannot find the top of it
I want to leave my sink
so filled up with dishes
I cannot see the bottom
I want to leave the filled hamper
and the empty refrigerator
I want to leave my messy closet
the unswept leaves
in front of the house
the buttons that need
to be sewn on
the hems that need
to be shortened
I want to leave the unmade bed
the dusty shelves
the unpressed shirts
the unanswered calls
the unpaid bills
the unwaxed floors
the unwashed windows
the TV that needs
to be fixed

Stop the world
I want to get off
at some other place
at some other time
where I can sit
without feeling guilty
doing nothing
an entire afternoon.

There Is Always One More Thing to Do

One more dish to wash
bed to make
laundry to put away

One more paper to file
letter to write
another bill to pay

One more pound to lose
book to read
video cassette to play

Just one more thing to do
every single day.

Sunday

I sit by my pool
sipping a Coke
with a scoop of chocolate ice cream

My feet in the sun
my head in the shade
my eyes on the distant horizon

I worked hard all week
I answered my mail
and my desk is not in a clutter

I called up my mother
talked to the kids
and straightened the drawers and closets

I sewed a loose button
tightened a screw
and threw out last Sunday's papers

I even made up
our bed today
although no company's coming

All this is to say
that I really deserve
that scoop of chocolate ice cream.

Hopeless Quest

Since I was twelve years old
I've been just one pound away
from being really beautiful
And even when I lose that pound
Somehow I'm always still
only one pound away
from being the "right" weight.

Diets

No bread
with strawberry jam
no rich desserts
no candy
no chocolate ice cream
no french fries
no chips

INSTEAD

carrot sticks
raw cauliflower
with a low-fat yogurt dip
broiled fish
cottage cheese
lettuce with a diet dressing
half a grapefruit
one salt-free cracker

Even if I don't live longer
it sure as hell will seem longer.

Thanksgiving Dinner

I don't really eat
turkey very often
nor sweet potatoes
nor cranberry sauce

I don't really like
big midday meals
nor bread stuffing
nor pumpkin pie

But I love
Thanksgiving dinner
with all the trimmings
and eating too much
all afternoon

And best of all
I love the leftovers.

Superstition

A black cat
     just crossed my path
My mother
     would have turned back

She throws salt
     over her shoulder
when she spills
     some at the table
she spits three times
     for good luck
never opens an umbrella
     in the house
does not admire
     a new baby
for fear of
     the evil eye
never puts
     shoes on a table
nor a hat
     on a bed
will not walk
     under a ladder
cannot whistle
     in the house
does not sit
     with her back to the door

nor seat thirteen
    at the table
cannot be third
    on a match
gets very upset
    when she breaks a mirror
I don't really
    believe in all this
although I read
    the astrological column
have charted
    my biorhythms
and have gone
    to fortune-tellers
without really
    believing in all this

But a black cat
    just crossed my path
Should I turn back?

Songs My Father Taught Me

My father sang me
Russian songs

they are the songs
I still remember

and when I hear them
I always cry.

Grandfather Likes to:

smoke a pipe
read his newspaper
listen to the radio
talk about politics
take an evening walk
around the block
tell Grandma what to do
and pat you on the head,
saying, "You're a good child."

First Bra

Lately when she runs downstairs
she has to hold her breasts
cupped in her hands
to keep them from bouncing

Her mother finally agreed
that she needed a brassiere
They went shopping and she tried on
small lacy ones
which she wanted
and thick cotton ones
which they bought

The next day in school
she was suddenly shy
wanting to hide
the two new protrusions
beneath her sweater
and hoping no one would notice
she was becoming a woman.

New Breasts

I remember feeling shy
about my growing breasts
wishing I could hold on to
my childhood a little longer

today's young girls
can't wait to have
breasts that show
announcing their womanhood.

Adolescence

She is in high school

She is in love
she speaks on the phone for hours
looks in the mirror endlessly
fixing her hair
trying on clothes
stuffing tissues in her bra

She is in love
she giggles incessantly
often making no sense at all
not doing her homework
eating junk food
smoking in secret

She is in love
she puts on too much makeup
had her ears pierced
goes to too many parties
and generally behaves
in ways I would consider crazy
were she not in high school

were she not in love.

First Wet Dream

He awakens from a strange dream
his bed dampened
by an unfamiliar substance
he remembers his father explaining
when this happened
he would be a man,
that he could have children now

he feels embarrassed though
in front of his mother
and washes his own sheets
hoping no one will notice.

My New Brother

When my brother was born
I was so excited
I was so thrilled
to have a baby brother
That happiness lasted for about ten minutes

I very quickly realized
that I had been demoted
from most loved special child
to just the sister of
that new miracle
the first male child.

Sibling

If you don't have a baby brother
you're dying to have one
pestering your parents
to make one for you

If you do have a little brother
you wish you were an only child
pestering your parents
to send him back
to wherever he came from.

The Telephone

When I'm alone
with nothing to do
or nowhere to go
I call members of my family
just to say hello
and talk for hours
on the phone

When they call me
it is like a gift
and I'm grateful

But when I'm busy
I don't call anyone
for days or even weeks
I have no time for them
no time for the phone
no time

If they call me
it's an intrusion
I secretly resent

Thank-You Note

You shouldn't have
it wasn't necessary
it's embarrassing
I wish you hadn't
Honestly!

Why did you?
you didn't have to
it's much too nice
you shouldn't have
Really!

I love it
it's a beautiful gift
and I'm so glad
you gave it to me
Thank you!

I Have a Cold

I have a bad cold
an ordinary garden-variety
awful kind of cold
with a sore throat
watery eyes
a stuffed-up nose
all red from blowing

I am *more* utterly, totally
absolutely miserable
when I have a cold
than I am ever
totally, utterly
absolutely delighted
when I don't.

Heat Wave

Damp arm pits
Sweat on my upper lip
Inner thighs
chafe against each other
My dress sticks to me
unpleasantly
no air

Dreaming of iced coffee
cold winter days
and snow.

Cold Wave

Eyes are watering
Nose is running
It hurts to breathe
Fingers are frozen
Toes are numb
I'm shivering and will
surely catch a cold

Dreaming of hot soup
warm summer days
and sun.

Appliances

My appliances
take up too much space
too much time
I cook faster
clean faster
write faster
get there faster
reach people faster
pushing buttons
turning dials
spinning my wheels
making my world
go even faster

past me.

The Computer

He bought a computer
to make life easier
he said
It sits on my desk
taking up room
I stare at this new complication
thinking that I have a food processor
but still chop with a knife
I have a dishwasher
but I wash by hand
I have a hairdryer
but prefer the sun
I have a microwave
but use the oven
I have a typewriter
but prefer longhand
I have an electric blanket
but my down quilt is cozier
I have a car
but I walk when I can
I have a vacuum
but use the broom
I have a television
but prefer to read
And now he bought me this computer
to make my life easier
he said.

Packing

Do I pack this
or throw it out?
A college diploma
I've kept it for thirty-five years
a high school medal
from a debating society
I was so proud to have won
a souvenir program
a ribbon
the photograph of an old beau
books I will never re-read
love letters
my children's paintings from kindergarten
an alligator bag I haven't worn in years
that still looks like new
old-fashioned dresses
that may someday
be back in style
a skirt that is too tight today
but will be fine when I lose weight

What do I re-pack
and take to the new house
What do I throw away
How does one decide?

It's not that I miss
what I don't own anymore
it's the parting of the ways
I find so difficult
the getting rid of things
that were once dear to me
but if it gives me pleasure
every few years to come across
some otherwise forgotten memory
why not put it back again
into the box
marked: "unpack last"
which means
it never gets unpacked at all
until the next move
when I will wonder again

Do I keep it?
Or throw it out?

Transportation

My grandmother
in her horse and carriage
did not travel far and wide
but on her way
she had time to look

My mother in her car
went a lot faster
but saw a lot less

I travel by plane
and see nothing at all.

Being Different

In France they called me the Russian girl
but I was born in Paris
it was my parents who were from Moscow

They called me the Jewish girl
when I attended the Catholic school
for I stood when the others knelt to pray

They called me the French girl
and laughed at my accent
at the school in New York

They called me the American woman
when I married in Europe
and lived in Lausanne

They called me the Swiss teacher
at the university
in New Hampshire

They called me the Easterner
when I moved to California

I was always the outsider
trying desperately to fit in
until finally now
I have learned to be comfortable
being me.

Mother by Memo

A memo on her desk

the doctor called,
"Congratulations,
your test is positive."

Her work project was her only baby
this baby will not be her only project.

The Happiest Day

Giving birth
to my first male child
overwhelmed me
with a strange primitive feeling
that I had just accomplished
a miracle
my body producing a being
totally different from myself.

Sick Child

My child is in the hospital
and my world is collapsing around me
my child is so sick
an awful panic fills my days
Will my child survive?

I talk with doctors
question nurses
trying to learn medical terms
understand prognoses
my stomach hurts
with my child away from me
and I promise myself
that never again shall I
worry about unimportant things
or get upset about
insignificant events.

I make secret deals with God
Let my child live!

Me Too!

I am always someone's daughter
someone's mother
someone's wife

I am also someone's teacher
someone's neighbor
someone's friend

I am available
responsible
can reliably be counted on

I wish I too had ME to lean on.

Adoptions

A seed blew onto
my windowsill

I planted it
gave it fertilizer
and just the right amount
of filtered light
sprayed it with water mist
on very dry days
even talked to it
when no one was listening
and as I watched it grow
and took care *of* it
I started caring *for* it
I grew very fond of my little plant

A puppy was left
on my doorstep

I fed it puppy food
and morsels from my dinner
gave it vitamins
took it to the vet
walked it on frosty mornings
and in the dark of night
trained it to heel
and come on command
and as I watched it grow
and took care *of* it
I started caring *for* it
I really liked my little puppy

A baby came
into my life

I fed him baby food
gave him vitamins
changed his diapers
took him to the doctor
played with him
sang him to sleep
taught him to say
"please" and "thank you"
and as I watched him grow
and took care *of* him
I started caring *for* him
I loved my little child

My seed has grown
into a lovely plant
that gives me joy
My puppy has become
a friendly dog
who guards my house
My baby is
a loving child
who fills my life.

Everyone Says:

I am the perfect mother
the model wife
the best housekeeper
the greatest cook
the most available daughter
the most effective worker
the most helpful friend

I am just wonderful
at everything
juggling home and career
with a constant smile
and an even disposition
I am everything everyone says
But who am I?

Stepchildren

Mine, but not really mine
his, but not his alone
not of my flesh,
but part of my family
sharing no genes
not sharing a name

Wanting to love
unconditionally
not always able to

Not quite a mother
not quite a friend
not an aunt
or a cousin

No title fits:
I am their father's wife.

Today's Parents

The baby has a fever
she can't go to day care
I tried to get a baby-sitter
none are available
I'm late for a meeting
can you call your mother?

> She's out of town this week
> I'm seeing customers
> can't take the baby with me
> can you stay home today?

Impossible, I'll lose my job
and you?

> I have appointments
> I cannot cancel
> Maybe the neighbor?

She's working too.

Perpetual Guilt

If I'm in the office
I wish I were home
with the children

If I'm home
with the children
I know I should be
in the office

I always should be
wherever I'm not.

My Favorite Woman

After we've spent the day together
we talk for hours on the phone
there is always more to say

She is the only person
I can comfortably shop with
and not feel impatient
when she tries on things forever
or worry that I'm taking too long
in deciding between two dresses

Only with her can I still giggle
mostly at the silliest things
I don't offer to shorten anyone else's hems
nor tidy up anyone else's kitchen
when she borrows something
I don't ask for it back

We exchange recipes
gossip about family members
and reminisce about the past

When she criticizes, it matters
her compliments mean more
than those of friends

She is my favorite woman to be with
I am talking about my daughter.

Shoelaces *

We were driving one day and my mother
said:

"You know, Nina,
in the last few years I've grown and
changed —
I'm feeling stronger —
I've been doing new things with my
life,
... have you noticed?"

You? Changed? — I never really looked.
you were always strong —
you rocked me to sleep
tied perfect shoelaces
knew how to multiply
worked
taught me how to put on
lipstick
traveled
had interesting conversations
with other adults
in the living room
(while I peeked from my
bedroom upstairs)

you always knew how to do things —
I was the one who was
learning.

and yet —

you know, Mom,
    in the last few years I've grown and
        changed —
    I'm feeling stronger —
    I've been doing new things with my
        life,
    ... I know you've noticed.

My daughter Laura
    doesn't know that I'm changing —
    I'm her mom
        who
        can already
        tie perfect shoelaces.

*A poem for me written by my daughter Nina

Ours and Theirs

Our kids are friendly
theirs have no manners

Our kids are creative
theirs are showing off

Our kids are outgoing
theirs are too noisy

Our kids fend for themselves
theirs are aggressive

Our kids show emotions
theirs are hysterical

Our kids love to talk
theirs won't shut up

Our kids know what they want
theirs are demanding

Our kids enjoy nice things
theirs are spoiled

Our kids are careful with money
theirs are stingy

Our kids feel close to us
theirs are too dependent

Our kids like sports
theirs are jocks

Our kids read books
theirs are eggheads

Our kids will do great things
theirs will not amount to much

Our kids are really special
theirs . . .

A No-Win Situation

If I were the kind of mother
who was dependent on her children
to call, to visit, to take care of her
they would resent it
and wish I were more self-sufficient

but I am the kind of mother
who has a busy life of her own
and not much time for the children
so they resent it
and complain that I'm not
more available.

Where Have All the Pretty Babies Gone?

All my friends had such cute children
we admired and applauded them
How charming, how precocious!

they're all adults now
with weight problems
or unruly beards
poor-paying jobs
and the wrong friends
either coming home too often
or else not calling enough

How disappointing!

The Split

Sometimes my heart
wants something so badly
but my head knows
that it is wrong

Sometimes my heart
longs for someone so much
but my head knows
that it's not right

My head says that
my heart is foolish
my heart says that
my head does not understand

And so I must live with
a heart and a head
who don't get along
doing what's wrong
while knowing
what's right.

The Maid

She cleans my house
changes my sheets
puts away dishes
washes my underwear

We talk a bit
of this and that
not too much
she is paid by the hour

She knows my life
in intimate detail
I don't know hers
and wonder how
she really feels

about

cleaning my house
changing my sheets
washing my underwear.

The Spa Experience

Carol says stretch
Jody says bend
Linda says lift
Suzanne says swing
Phyllis says breathe
Margaret says don't eat

I stand at the back
of the exercise class
hoping no one will notice
that I can't sit
with my legs straight
can't touch my toes
can't straighten my back
can't bend sideways

On the morning walk
I fall behind
the seventy-year-old lady
and the six-year-old child

I am first only
in the dining room.

The Bus Tour

Look to the right
a snow-covered mountain
look to the left
you just missed a moose
straight ahead
a bald eagle
Where?
That spot on the tree
Where are the binoculars?

To the left
a waterfall
to the right
a stream
we stop for a ten-minute stretch
Where is the ladies' room?

Look to the right
a towering peak
look to the left
a glacier
straight ahead
an elk on the road
Where is the camera?

Look to the right
no, to the left
look, look
while the landscape flashes by
too quickly
Where are the memories?

The Oyster River

The first night in the new house
we thought it was raining
but when we looked out it had not
The second night we heard again
the sound of water falling
but all was dry outside

The river had swelled
from the melting spring snows
Just under our window
a small rushing waterfall
was splashing over rocks

The river was fast
bumping along big tree stumps
as it flowed downstream
It was maybe twenty feet wide
and deep enough to drown me

Then the summer came
and the river trickled
We could not hear it at night
as we walked across its bed easily
and fished in the quiet pools

The autumn laid leaves upon it
and I watched them sail slowly by
The river was narrow
with only six feet
to the other side

The winter iced it completely
except for one pool near the rocks
When the snow fell over the river
we cross-country skied its full length
from Mill Road to the Mill Pond

Every morning before breakfast
I check to see if the river is still there
and with floodlights after sunset
we can still watch it in the dark

The river has become a presence
someone who lives with us
When people come to visit
we say
oh, come look at *our* river today!

My Son Called

A baby moved today
in utero
for the first time
they felt it move
they called across two continents
to say
the baby moved today.

Falling in Love with a Baby

I saw my tough, cool, macho son
fall in love with a baby this week

I saw my somewhat arrogant son
come apart when the baby cried this week

I saw my son melt with tenderness
when he watched the baby nursing this week

I saw my son overcome with joy
when the baby smiled in his sleep this week

I saw my rather fastidious son
change a diaper this week

I saw my son
become a father this week.

Nicholas

His mouth is his father's
his eyes are his mother's
his nose is his cousin's
his toes are his aunt's
his grandfather says
he looks just like he did
when he was a little boy
and has an old photo to prove it
I only know that
he's the most beautiful baby
I have ever seen
and he's not like any of them
he's just like his grandmother:
me.

Unconditional Love

My son looked at
his newborn
in my arms
and said:
"Do you love me
the way I love him?"
and I said,
"Yes,"
and he said,
"Amazing!"

Important Phone Calls

When my son
took his first steps
I called my mother
long distance
to tell her

Today,
thirty years later,
my son's child
took his first steps
he called me
to tell me
long distance

and I called
my mother
again.

Welcome to the World

My grandson
loves books
looks intently at paintings
noticing the smallest detail
his eyes wide open
to *see* the world

My other grandson
loves music
listens intently to sound
noticing every noise
his ears wide open
to *hear* the world

My granddaughter
loves action
must do everything herself
touching people and objects
her arms wide open
to *grasp* the world.

Two and a Half

Two and a half
She won't play by herself
"Grandma, I need you"

Two and a half
A person with preferences
"Play with me, Grandma"

Two and a half
She likes apple juice
better than milk

Won't wear her blue sweater
won't get her hair brushed
wants to go out RIGHT NOW

"Don't talk on the phone, Grandma
Why can't I have your lipstick
I don't want to go to bed
I'm not sleepy"

But Grandma is tired
"No you're not
Read me a story
Sing me a song

I need more water
Grandma, I love you
I give you a big big hug"

I guess Grandma isn't so tired after all.

My Grandchild Is a Genius

When Laura surprises me by saying
"please" and "thank you"
it seems that this is normal
for a three-year-old

When Laura amazes me
by offering me her cookie
it seems all three-year-olds
do that too

When Laura sings a song
almost right in tune
no one seems to find it
extraordinary

When Laura twirls around
in rhythm to the music
no one stops to watch her
with much admiration

Except her grandmother.

Super-Grandma Guilt

She thought the guilt would leave
when the children grew up
but now it has returned
when the grandchildren visit

No turkey in the oven
no apron round her waist
no infant in her arms
not for long anyway
not available to baby-sit
nor spend an afternoon
with children in the playground
Grandma has a meeting,
a project to be finished,
a deadline, a conference call,

Grandma has a career!

They Don't Do It Right

Why aren't my children
raising their children
the way that *they* were raised!

Those babies should not be given hot dogs
should drink more milk, not apple juice
should not be naked when it's chilly
should not crayon in the living room
should not grab from other children
not touch every item in the store
not leave the table during mealtime
not watch TV as much as they do

Those babies should say "please" and
                    "thank you"
be still, be quiet, play by themselves
not be demanding nor capricious
have fewer tantrums
far fewer toys

But I say nothing
just sigh in silence
and wonder,

How come I did not raise my children
to raise their children
the way that they were raised?

The Children Visit

I'm so excited
I can't wait
they're coming soon

I cleaned the house
put flowers in their room
bought their favorite foods
canceled my classes
told friends I would be busy

It was wonderful
It was exhausting

And now
I'm so excited
I can't wait
they're leaving soon.

Out of Trouble, Out of Mind

When my daughter's in pain
I hurt too
When my son is sick
I don't feel well
When my grandchild
has problems
I'm distressed

When all is well
I don't think about them that much.

Not Me

In the first part of life
my growing children
cramped my style

In the second part of life
my aging parents
cramp my style

In the last part of life
I could not possibly of course
ever cramp my children's style!

Visiting My Mother

I had arrived before lunch
spent the afternoon with her
had dinner together
then for a short time
I went off to see a friend

When I returned
she was more upset
that I had left her
for an hour
than she was glad
that I had come
for the whole day.

No Exit

If I don't have enough work
I get anxious
so I accept more to do
and then I have too much
and I get harried
and so I try to do less
but then I don't have enough
to keep me busy
so I get depressed
and I increase my work load
but then I can't manage it all
and I become frantic
so I decrease my responsibilities
and don't have enough work
so I get anxious . . .

Categories

"All women do"
but some may not
"All men are"
but a few are not
"Most women would think"
but "no man would say"
What are these categories
for anyway?
I am just a small part
of a large percentage
a statistic
a number
a class
A woman who
is middle-aged
white
has children
works in a traditional female job
teaching
in a non-traditional female setting
business
A woman who
takes vitamins
diets

has low-blood pressure
yearly checkups
lives in a house
on top of a hill
goes to bed early
does not exercise
reads *Newsweek*
likes movies
is well-organized
most of the time
A woman who
gets nervous
before trips
does not smoke
uses liquid soap
writes verse
A woman who
is part of a category
of women who
are just like that.
I prefer thinking
there's only one of me
in that particular
category.

Sometimes I Am Unhappy

Sometimes
I am unhappy
for no reason
at all

I try to count
my blessings:
a nice home
a loving husband
healthy kids
a good job

and still
I feel dissatisfied
restless
listless
irritated

I ask myself
what's the matter with me
I should be grateful
for all I have
I don't even know
what's missing

Yet some days
I am unhappy
for no reason
at all.

Not Here

A nuclear reactor
ought to be built
but not in my state

All toxic wastes
should have dumping sites
but not in my county

Off-shore drilling
may be necessary
but not near my shores

A new jail is needed
to decrease overcrowding
but not in my town

A home for the retarded
would be a good thing
but not on my block

Minority people
can live anywhere
but not in my building

I agree with it all
as long as it's there
and not here.

Tragedy Under the Eaves

Every year the swallows come
and build their nests of clay
right under the roof of my bedroom window
we know one another
and watch one another
throughout the summer months

today I found two eggs
splattered on the ground
pushed out by a pair of finches
who now are nesting
in their stolen home

I don't care that it is called
survival of the fittest
I'm angry and upset
and say it is not right

though it's really very silly of me
to expect more from birds
than I expect from people.

Compliments?

He said
you must have been pretty
when you were young

She said
I won't mind growing older
if I look like you

They said
it's nice to have you
as an older role model

And I said
Who me?

Middle Age

Being in between
parents who have become like children
and need you
and children who are still just that
and need you.

Cardiogram

My mother's cardiogram
was not good
I was surprised and shocked
I thought she would live forever
and always be there for me
she had *promised* it!

but her cardiogram is not good
I will never be ready to be
without a mother

Mothers should not
make promises
they cannot keep.

When I Was Little

When I was little
I depended on my mother
she nursed me
when I was sick
took me to the doctor
and told me not to worry
she would always be there
to take care of me

And now that I'm grown
and my mother is old
she depends on me
to nurse her when she's sick
take her to the doctor
and tell her not to worry
I'll always be there
to take care of her.

Not Just Yet

First my grandparents,
now my parents, aunts and uncles
are dying one by one
They are the buffer generation
between me and death

When they are gone,
I will be next in line
In this queue
I would gladly
let others
get ahead of me
this is one queue where
I won't push my way
to get to the front
but rather stand way back
as inconspicuously
as possible

Hoping Death
will not notice me
not just yet.

Just Being There

When his son died
it ripped his gut
and left a gash
that wouldn't heal

when his son died
it crippled him
and left him limping
all alone

when his son died
I watched him suffer
but had no words
that could have helped

when his son died
I just stood by
until he noticed
that I was there.

Memory Loss

So much information
is thrown at us
that it is no wonder
some of it bounces
right off our brains
without leaving a trace.

Not Alzheimer's

The young people don't worry when

they don't remember
their best friend's name,

lose their car keys twice a week,

can't find their wallets,

misplace their glasses,

walk into a room
and not know what it was
they were looking for,

forget their own phone numbers,

can't think of a common word
they use every day,

can't recall what they just read
or what someone just said,

lose the list of things to remember,

the young people just shrug their
shoulders but the older people think
they have Alzheimer's disease.

To My Visitor

Older can be lonely
older can be forgotten
older can be "who cares?"

Older can be difficult
difficult to walk unaided
difficult to chew
difficult to see
difficult to hear
to get out of bed
in the morning

Older can be worthwhile
if somebody cares.

Older Is Better

Older is wiser
older does not fret
over little things
has no small children
to worry about
has adjusted well to a mate
or to life without one
can pursue interests
shelved in youth
have new leisure
with new hobbies

Older is easier
does not have to impress
anyone anymore
is asked advice of
given seats in buses
is respected and sought after
does not worry about face-lifts
or dyeing grey hair

Older is an arrival place
where there is time for passion
and time for contemplation
and time to enjoy time.

Progress

I looked for some patterns
last week
to make two needlepoint pillows
one for my granddaughter
and one for my grandson
The pictures all showed
little girls
cooking or sewing
and little boys
skating or fishing
I guess nothing
has really changed
after all.

Roads Not Taken

I was looking forward
to a quiet evening at home
curled up with a book

and then he called
and said there was
this really great movie
and we really ought to go

I was looking forward
to a quiet life by the beach
curled up with my love

and then they called
and said there was
this great opportunity
and I really ought to go

I'm sorry they called
because now
I must make a decision.
By having a choice
I have lost
my peace of mind

Sometimes you should refuse
the offer you can't refuse.

PMZ*

You have to be old enough
and have had a lot of experience
to be wise enough
to understand
that although in our youth
we had a lot of energy
it was dissipated
on many pursuits
spread out over
many people

but now at an older age
we have energy
well-focused on
a few important undertakings
energy directed at
a few significant people

those older years are the very best
when you have °Post-Menopausal Zest.

Families

Families may be those
who have borne you
and families may be those
who have grown you
Families may be those
who have known you
But no matter what you do
real families
will never disown you.